MOBILE SUIT GUNDAM SEED

VOLUME 2

ART BY
Masatsugu Iwase
ORIGINAL STORY BY
Hajime Yatate AND Yoshiyuki Tomino

TRANSLATED AND ADAPTED BY

Jason DeAngelis

LETTERED BY

Steve Palmer

DEL REY

BALLANTINE BOOKS · NEW YORK

A Del Rey® Book
Published by The Random House Publishing Group

Published in the United States by Del Rey Books, an imprint of The Random
House Publishing Group, a division of Random House, Inc., New York, and
simultaneously in Canada by Random House of Canada Limited, Toronto. First
published in serialization and subsequently published in book form by Kodansha,
Ltd., Tokyo in 2003.

www.delreymanga.com

Library of Congress Control Number can be obtained from the
publisher upon request.

ISBN 0-345-47179-2

Translator and adaptor—Jason DeAngelis
Lettering—Steve Palmer
Cover design—David Stevenson

Manufactured in the United States of America

First Edition: September 2004

3 4 5 6 7 8 9

Contents

Honorifics Explained

Throughout the Del Rey Manga books, you will find Japanese honorifics left intact in the translations. For those not familiar with how the Japanese use honorifics, and, more important, how they differ from American honorifics, we present this brief overview.

Politeness has always been a critical facet of Japanese culture. Ever since the feudal era, when Japan was a highly stratified society, use of honorifics—which can be defined as polite speech that indicates relationship or status—has played an essential role in the Japanese language. When addressing someone in Japanese, an honorific usually takes the form of a suffix attached to one's name (e.g. "Asuna-san"), as a title at the end of one's name, or in place of the name itself (e.g. "Negi-sensei" or simply "Sensei!").

Honorifics can be expressions of respect or endearment. In the context of manga and anime, honorifics give insight into the nature of the relationship between characters. Many translations into English leave out these important honorifics, and therefore distort the feel of the original Japanese. Because Japanese honorifics contain nuances that English honorifics lack, it is our policy at Del Rey not to translate them. Here, instead, is a guide to some of the honorifics you may encounter in Del Rey Manga.

-san: This is the most common honorific and is equivalent to Mr., Miss, Ms., Mrs, etc. It is the all-purpose honorific and can be used in any situation where politeness is required.

-sama: This is one level higher than -san. It is used to confer great respect.

-dono: This comes from the word *tono*, which means *lord*. It is an even higher level than -sama and confers utmost respect.

-kun: This suffix is used at the end of boys' names to express familiarity or endearment. It is also sometimes used by men among friends, or when addressing someone younger or of a lower station.

-chan: This is used to express endearment, mostly toward girls. It is also used for little boys, pets, and between lovers. It gives a sense of childish cuteness.

Bozu: This is an informal way to refer to a boy, similar to the English term "kid" or "squirt."

Sempai: This title suggests that the addressee is one's senior in a group or organization. It is most often used in a school setting, where underclassmen refer to their upperclassmen as *sempai*. It can also be used in the workplace, such as when a newer employee addresses an employee who has seniority in the company.

Kohai: This is the opposite of *-sempai*, and is used toward underclassmen in school or newcomers in the workplace. It connotes that the addressee is of a lower station.

Sensei: Literally meaning "one who has come before," this title is used for teachers, doctors, or masters of any profession or art.

-[blank]: This is usually forgotten on these lists, but it's perhaps the most significant difference between Japanese and English. The lack of honorific means that the speaker has permission to address the person in a very intimate way. Usually, only family, spouses, or very close friends have this kind of license. Known as *yobisute*, it can be gratifying when someone who has earned the intimacy starts to call one by one's name without an honorific. But when that intimacy hasn't been earned, it can also be insulting.

機動戦士ガンダム SEED シード

MOBILE SUIT GUNDAM

STORY:
HAJIME YATATE AND
YOSHIYUKI TOMINO

ART:
MASATSUGU IWASE

THE STORY SO FAR

71 C.E. (COSMIC ERA). IN THE AFTERMATH OF THE "BLOODY VALENTINE," THE WAR BETWEEN EARTH ALLIANCE FORCES AND THE ZAFT DRAGGED ON AND ELEVEN MONTHS HAD PASSED. KIRA YAMATO, A STUDENT ON SPACE COLONY HELIOPOLIS, BELONGING TO THE NEUTRAL NATION OF AUBE, BECOMES EMBROILED IN THE ZAFT'S PLAN TO CAPTURE THE EARTH'S NEW MOBILE SUITS, AND IS FORCED TO PILOT THE X-105 STRIKE GUNDAM AND REPEL THE ZAFT FORCES. HOWEVER, AFTER BEING EXPOSED TO MILITARY SECRETS, KIRA AND HIS RESCUED FRIENDS END UP STUCK ABOARD THE EARTH FORCES' NEW BATTLESHIP ARCHANGEL. ZAFT'S COMMANDER CREUSET, WHO CAPTURED FOUR OF THE FIVE NEW MOBILE SUITS, LAUNCHES AN ATTACK ON THE ARCHANGEL. AND KIRA, ALTHOUGH RELUCTANT TO FIGHT, BOARDS THE STRIKE YET AGAIN, REALIZING THAT AS A COORDINATOR, HE IS THE ONLY ONE WHO CAN DEFEND HIS FRIENDS. IN THE MIDST OF BATTLE, KIRA COMES ACROSS HIS OLD FRIEND ATHRUN, WHO PILOTS THE STOLEN X-303 AEGIS. BOTH ARE SHOCKED AT THEIR CURRENT PREDICAMENT. MEANWHILE, THE BATTLE ESCALATES, AND HELIOPOLIS IS DESTROYED. COMMANDER CREUSET PURSUES THE ARCHANGEL AS IT HEADS FOR THE EARTH BASE ON THE MOON. KIRA FIGHTS DESPERATELY TO PROTECT HIS FRIENDS, AND IGNORES ATHRUN'S APPEALS, WHICH HE KNOWS WITHIN HIS HEART ARE WRONG. SUDDENLY, THERE'S TROUBLE IN THE ARCHANGEL ENGINES! NOW, DRAGGED BY THE EARTH'S GRAVITATIONAL FIELD TOWARD THE PERILOUS "DEBRIS BELT," FILLED WITH SPACE JUNK AND WRECKAGE, THEY ARE HEADED FOR CERTAIN DEATH. OR ARE THEY?

GAT-X105 STRIKE GUNDAM
THE NEWEST MOBILE WEAPONRY (MOBILE SUIT) DEVELOPED ON HELIOPOLIS BY EARTH ALLIANCE FORCES. ABLE TO CONFIGURE INTO THREE DIFFERENT MODES: AILE, SWORD, AND LAUNCHER.

KIRA YAMATO
A COORDINATOR WHO, FLEEING THE RAVAGES OF WAR, TOOK REFUGE IN HELIOPOLIS. HIS PARENTS ARE NATURALS. FORCED TO PILOT THE STRIKE DUE TO HIS SUPERIOR ABILITIES.

ATHRUN ZALA
A COORDINATOR WHO WAS KIRA'S BEST FRIEND AT THE LUNAR PREPARATORY SCHOOL. AS A VOLUNTEER TO ZAFT FORCES, HE IS ASSIGNED TO THE CREUSET TEAM. PILOT OF THE AEGIS.

VOOOON

MY
PHAS
SHIF
IS...

....DOWN!!

UWAAAAAA!!

WAM!

!!

HAHH...
HAHH...

IT SEEMS THE BOMBARDED NAZCA CLASS HAS WITHDRAWN FROM THIS SECTOR.

STATUS OF ENEMY SHIPS?

THE RASIA-LASS GATE IS NG US UST SIDE OF FIRING NGE.

ENSIGN BAD-GIRUEL!

WE CAN SHAKE OFF THAT LAURASIA-CLASS IF WE GET THIS SHIP UP TO TOP SPEED!!

HURRY UP WITH THOSE BLASTED ENGINE REPAIRS!

I CAN'T BELIEVE IT...AT THIS RATE, IT'S UNLIKELY WE'LL EVER GET RESUPPLIED...

BUT THEY'RE ALSO WORKING ON THE STRIKE AND ZERO... AND THERE'S A SHORTAGE OF MANPOWER...

I'M TRYING TO SPEED THINGS UP!!

WE STILL HAVE OUR EMERGENCY RATIONS, SO WE'RE FINE WITH FOOD...

THE PROBLEM IS AMMUNITION AND WATER.

WHAT IS IT, ENSIGN?

NO... IT'S JUST THAT...

WE'RE NOT SHORT ON FOOD, ARE WE?

IS THERE SOME SORT OF PROBLEM ENSIGN BAD-GIRUEL?

WATER. I SEE....

HM?!

WAIT A SEC... I KNOW JUST THE PLACE TO GET FRESH SUPPLIES!

!

RIGHT WHERE THIS SHIP IS HEADED.

SHOOOM

YOU DON'T MEAN... THE DEBRIS BELT?!

RIGHT WHERE WE'RE HEADED ...?

TOLLE...

DIDN'T YOU SEE THE LAST BATTLE?!

KIRA'S NOT THE ENEMY!!

IT WAS KIRA WHO RESCUED THE ESCAPE POD THAT YOU WERE IN.

BUT...

FLAY... KIRA IS A COORDINATOR, BUT HE'S NOT ZAFT.

WELL... IF YOU SAY SO...

I GUARANTEE IT.

.....

BUT IN THE EARTH FORCES, IT'S A BIT OF A PROBLEM...

WE MAY HAVE ACCEPTE THAT KIRA'S COORDIN TOR...

HE WAS MY FRIEND AT THE LUNAR PREPARATORY SCHOOL. HE'S A COORDINATOR.

THE FINAL UNIT... THE PERSON PILOTING IT WAS NONE OTHER THAN KIRA YAMATO.

AN UNEXPECTED INCIDENT...?

I'LL MAKE SURE TO SUBMIT A REPORT IMMEDIATELY.

I'M SORRY... I WAS LATE TO REPORT IT.

I SEE... THAT EXPLAINS YOUR IRREGULAR BEHAVIOR EVER SINCE HELIOPOLIS...

HUH?

THAT WON'T BE NECESSARY.

BUT ALSO BECAUSE WE'VE BEEN ORDERED TO APPEAR BEFORE AN INQUIRY COMMISSION INVESTIGATING THE DESTRUCTION OF HELIOPOLIS...

THIS SHIP IS RETURNING HOME FOR NOW. NOT ONLY FOR SUPPLIES AN REPAIRS...

?!

BUT BEAR THIS IN MIND...

IT MIGHT BE A BIT INCONVENIENT.

IF WE BRING UP THE FACT THAT ONE OF THE ENEMY PILOTS WAS A COORDINATOR...

IF HE'S THE ENEMY, YOU MUST DESTROY HIM!

EVEN IF YOUR OPPONENT IS A FORMER FRIEND, IT MATTERS NOT...

YES SIR...

BUT...

IF HE ONLY REALIZES THE FACT THAT HE'S JUST BEING USED BY THE NATURALS...

B-BUT HE'S A COORDINATOR TOO! IF WE JUST TALK TO HIM, HE MAY COME AROUND TO OUR SIDE!

!!

IF HE'S NOT WILLING TO LISTEN, WHAT THEN?

I-IN THAT CASE....

IN...THAT CASE...

ATHRUN...

I'LL KILL HIM!

....KIRA....

YES SIR!

I'M IMPRESSED WITH YOUR RESOLVE. I'M COUNTING ON YOU.

HMM....

LIEUTENANT FLAGA!

SERGEA[N]... HAVE YO[U] SEEN TH[E] KID?

WHY ARE YOU IN THE EARTH FORCES?!

HUH?

KASHA KASHA

HE'S JUST BEEN SITTING IN THE COCKPIT OF THE STRIKE FOR THE PAST THREE HOURS...

......

KID...

?!

KIRA!

WHY ARE YOU FIGHTING FOR THE NATURALS?!

?!

NOBODY CAN DO THAT SORT OF THING EXCEPT KIRA.

WELL... WHAT IF YOU SEARCH THROUGH ALL THE ELECTRONIC LOCK NUMBERS...

?

SAI... TOLLE... KUZZEY...?

WAAUGH!! KIRA! LIEUTENANT FLAGA!!

?!

WHAT ARE YOU GUYS UP TO?

USUALLY, SEXUAL HARASSMENT ON A BATTLESHIP RESULTS IN A COURT MARTIAL!!

FOR A MILITARY MAN, NO, FOR ANYONE AT ALL... PEEPIN' IS A DESPICABLE ACT!

BUT WE CAN'T JUST OVERLOOK THE FACT THAT—

THAT'S ENOUGH, ENSIGN.

EH!! A C-COURT MARTIAL?!

AND NOW THAT WE'RE ABOUT TO PLUNGE INTO THE DEBRIS BELT, WE REALLY DON'T HAVE TIME FOR SUCH TRIVIALITIES.

THEIR BEHAVIOR WAS CERTAINLY IMMODEST, BUT THEY'RE REALLY NOT OFFICIAL SOLDIERS.

THAT PLACE FULL OF SPACE WRECKAGE FROM THE GRAVITATIONAL PULL...?

THE DEBRIS BELT... FOR REAL...?

ALERT, 360 DEGREES, ALL DIRECTIONS. WATCH OUT FOR ALL DEBRIS!

THE ARCHANGEL IS NOW ENTERING THE DEBRIS BELT!

WATER, FOOD, AMMUNITION... IT'S GOT EVERYTHING...

LIEUTENANT FLAGA'S RIGHT. IF WE LOOK AT IT DIFFERENTLY, THE DEBRIS BELT IS A TREASURE TROVE...

CAPTAIN! LARGE OBJECT SIGHTED AHEAD...!!

BUT... TAKING SOMETHING THAT ISN'T OURS...

?!

ISN'T THAT THE SAME AS ROBBING A DEAD MAN OF HIS VALUABLES...?

?!

WH-WHAT
IS IT...?!

IT'S ALMOST
LIKE A
GRAVE
MARKER IN
SPACE...

I'VE HEARD
THAT THE
WRECKAGE OF
JUNIUS SEVEN
DRIFTED INTO
THE DEBRIS
BELT...

ARE YOU SERIOUS ?!

YOU'RE SAYING WE SHOULD TAKE OUR SUPPLIES FROM THAT PLACE...!!

WHEN YOU SAY JUNIUS SEVEN, YOU MEAN THE SITE OF THE "BLOODY VALENTINE

JUST WATER AND SOME PARTS FOR REPAIRS...

WE'LL ONLY TAKE WHAT'S NECESSARY...

NO ONE'S SUGGESTING THAT WE'RE GOING TO ACT LIKE GRAVE ROBBERS!

IN THAT CASE, WE REALLY HAVE NO CHOICE...

WATER ...

KID!

IS THIS HOW THE EARTH FORCES CONDUCTS ITSELF?!

THAT'S JUST A RATIONALIZATION!

AND END UP LIKE THAT INSTEAD...?

OR PERHAPS YOU WOULD RATHER KEEP YOUR HANDS CLEAN...

TO STAY ALIVE, SOMETIMES YOU GOT TO DO THINGS WHICH ARE NOT ALWAYS PRETTY!

RIGHT NOW, WE'RE ALIVE!

......

?!

FATHER!

AH... I MEAN...

YEAH... YOU TOO...

IT'S AN HONOR TO SEE YOU AGAIN!

NATIONAL DEFENSE CHAIRMAN ZALA!

HOW AWKWARD...

HM... IN PUBLIC THEY HAVE TO ACT LIKE THEY'RE NOT FATHER AND SON...

THE DEBRIS BELT?!

THE GAMOW HAS REPORTEDLY LOST ITS PREY IN THE VICINITY OF THE DEBRIS BELT.

?!

COMMANDER!

FIRST OFF, RAU LE CREUSET!

LET'S HEAR YOUR REPORT.

WE SHALL NOW COMMENCE THE EMERGENCY INQUIRY COMMISSION INTO THE DESTRUCTION OF THE AUBE UNION'S COLONY HELIOPOLIS.

YES SIR!

KIRA...

OUR INTENTIONS WERE NEVER TO ATTACK HELIOPOLIS ITSELF...

WHY ARE YOU IN THE EARTH FORCES ...?

THERE IS NO ONE HERE WHO WISHES TO FIGHT!!

WE WISH TO LIVE IN PEACE AND QUIET... THAT IS OUR ONLY HOPE...

WHO AMONG US ENJOYS GOING TO WAR?

CHAIRMA ZALA...

.....

WHO HAS CONTINUED TO EXPLOIT US, SUPPRESSING US FOR THEIR OWN PERSONAL GAIN AND DESIRE?!

BUT WHO IS IT THAT HA BRUTALL SMASHE. THAT HOPE?!

WE MUST NEVER FORGET...

THE TRAGEDY OF THE "BLOODY VALENTINE" ON JUNIUS SEVEN!!

WAM!

243,721...
THAT'S HOW MANY
COORDINATORS
WERE LOST ON
THAT HORRIFIC
DAY...

WE FIGHT IN
ORDER TO
PROTECT
OUR-
SELVES!!

IF FIGHTING
IS THE ONLY
WAY WE CAN
SURVIVE...
THEN FIGHT
WE MUST!!

HEH-
HEH....

...FATHER
...

IT'S BEEN AWHILE, HONORABLE CHAIRMAN.

HEY, ATHRUN.

SHE SENT ME MAIL TO TELL ME SHE WAS GOING TO VISIT JUNIUS SEVEN WITH HER MEMORIAL SERVICE TROOP.

WHAT A SHAME. YOU'RE FINALL BACK, AND NO MY DAUGHTER LACUS IS AWA WORKING.

?!

HONOR-ABLE CHAIR-MAN!

YOU NEVER SEEM TO GET THE CHANCE TO SEE EACH OTHER...

ENGAGE TO BE MARRIE AND YET

!!

IT'S BEEN REPORTED THAT THE MEMORIAL SERVICE SHIP HAS DISAPPEARED IN THE VICINITY OF THE DEBRIS BELT...

VOHHHHHH

HOW MUCH LONGER?

NGINE
AIRS
RE
PLETE.

KA
KA
KA
KA

HOW IS THE INSPECTION OF JUNIUS SEVEN PROCEEDING, ENSIGN BAD-GIRUEL?

ALL WE NEED IS FOUR MORE HOURS TO EXTRACT THE ICE AND OTHER MATERIALS...

IT'S NEARLY IN PERFECT CONDITION THIS FAR IN.

I'M GOING A LITTLE FARTHER IN.

WE HAVEN'T FOUND ANYTHING YET THAT APPEARS USEFUL.

?!

KYAAA!!

?!

THEY MUST HAVE BEEN TRYING TO GET IN BUT IT WAS FULL...

THEY'RE BLOCKING THE ENTRANCE TO THE SHELTER...

WHAT IS IT?!

ENSIGN, OVER HERE!!

W-WHAT HAPPENED ...?

....

LOOK'S LIKE THEY COMMITTED GROUP SUICIDE BEFORE THEY RAN OUT OF OXYGEN...

THE ENEMY?!

BEEEP!

I...I CAN'T BELIEVE WE'RE DOING THIS...EVEN IF WE'RE AT WAR...

WHERE?!

A LONG-RANGE RECONNAIS-SANCE GINN?!

A CIVILIAN SHIP... IT'S BEEN HIT...?

?!

THE ARCHANGEL IS IMMOBILE...

IF IT'S DISCOVERED AND REINFORCEMENTS ARE CALLED...

COULD THAT BE... THE PILOT...?!

IT'S A WOMAN ...?!

AM... AT WAR... AND I MUST KILL...?

THAT'S RIGHT... PEOPLE WERE INSIDE THOSE MOBILE SUITS THAT I DESTROYED BEFORE...

I DON'T WANT TO KILL NYMORE...

DON'T MAKE ME SHOOT YOU DOWN...

GO! GET OUT OF HERE...

GREAT!

VOHHH

PLEASE...

DON'T
COME
OUT
!!

FOO
!!

STOP
!!

UWAA
AAAA
!!

PLEASE,
DON'T
!!

ARE YOU OKAY, KIRA?!

......

THANK YOU... FOR SAVING ME... KIRA... KIRA?

BEEP

I....DIDN'T WANT TO... SHOOT IT DOWN...

UGGH... I....

?!

BEEP
BEEP
ピッ
ピッ

A LIFEPOD...

?!

YOU AND YOUR LIFEPODS. THIS IS STARTING TO BECOME A HABIT.

A ONE-MAN LIFEPOD... AND THE FACT THAT A GINN CAME THIS FAR TO SEARCH FOR IT...

OPENING ...

PSHOO

THERE MUST BE AN IMPORTANT ZAFT PERSONAGE ONBOARD...

RELATED TO SIEGEL CLYNE, SUPREME CHAIRMAN OF THE ZAFT COUNCIL?!

LACUS... CLYNE?!

THIS IS A ZAFT SHIP, RIGHT...?

MY NAME IS LACUS CLYNE.

EH...?!

LOOKS LIKE YOU BROUGHT IN ANOTHER HELLUVA GAL...

HARO

HARO

?

PHASE-06 END

PHASE-07 THE ENEMY SONGSTRESS

RELATED TO SIEGEL CLYNE, SUPREME CHAIRMAN OF THE ZAFT COUNCIL?!

LACUS... CLYNE...?!

SIEGEL CLYNE IS MY FATHER.

?

!!

WHAT'S UP?

HARO

HARO

THIS IS MY FRIEND HARO.

CRAP! THANKS TO HER AND HER KIND, HELIOPOLIS IS GONE...

THERE GOES THE DAUGHTER OF THE ZAFT'S TOP DOG.

?

WE'RE AT WAR BECAUSE YOU COORDINATORS EXIST!

?

UGH......

PLEASE DON'T TRY TO LEAVE THIS ROOM

THANK YOU.

IF THERE'S ANYTHING ELSE YOU NEED, JUST USE THAT INTERCOM OVER THERE...

I'LL LEAVE YOUR FOOD HERE. I'LL COME AND TAKE YOUR TRAY LATER.

AND THERE ARE SOME PEOPLE ONBOARD WHO DON'T LOOK TOO KINDLY ON COORDINATORS...

I'M SORRY... THIS IS AN EARTH FORCES SHIP...

I'M REALLY NOT ALLOWED OUTSIDE?

BUT YOU'RE KIND TO ME.

?!

BECAUSE I'M A COORDI- NATOR TOO...

....

NO... YOU'RE N TO ME BECAU THAT'S THE KI OF PERSON YOU ARE.

HARO HARO.

SHALL WE SING SOME- THING, HARO?

HEE HEE...

EH....?!

OF ALL PEOPLE, SIEGEL CLYNE'S DAUGHTER... THIS PUTS US IN A BIT OF A JAM.

......

I-IT HASN'T BEEN DETERMINED YET IF IT WAS THE EARTH FORCES THAT ATTACKED THE SHIP...!

ACCORDING TO HER, THE MEMORIAL SERVICE TROOP SHIP WAS ATTACKED BY EARTH FORCES...

UH... WHAT'S THIS...?!

NATURALLY, WE'LL BE THE ONES WHO ARE SUSPECT...

WE'RE RECEIVING AN EARTH FORCES ENCRYPTION PULSE!

WHAT IS IT...?

IT'S...FROM THE EIGHTH FLEET!!

CAN'T YOU GET IT CLEARER?

THE RADIO INTERFERENCE IS SEVERE...

ARCHAN... *CRAK...* RECONNAI-SANCE... ATTACKED BY ZAFT SHIPS... ASSISTANCE REQUEST-ED... *BZZ BZTT...*

RAK CRAK.. FLAGS OF TH EIGHTH FLEET. MONT. MERY..

?!

THE GINN... *KRAK...* CAN'T SHOOT IT DOWN...

...

GO TO IT!

WE BETTER LAUNCH THE ZERO AND STRIKE!

THAT VOICE IT'S FLAY"

C'MON, LET'S GO!

I... I WILL... I PROMISE HE'LL BE OKAY....

I'M FIGHTING TO PROTECT... AND TO SAVE FLAY'S FATHER.

I'M NOT FIGHTING IN ORDER TO KILL...

KIRA YAMATO. PROCEED TO CATAPULT LAUNCH.

KLANK

BLAST OFF !!

KIRA YAMATO! STRIKE GUNDAM !!

VOOOOSHHH

KA-BLAM

ESCORT SHIP LAW UNDER FIRE!!

BLAM

BLAM

IT'S REALLY NOT THE TIME FOR THIS...

WHAT'S THE COMMANDER THINKING...?

X-303 AEGIS IS HEADING TOWARD THE BERNARD!!

THE AEGIS IS TRANS- FORMING!!

KLANK

SHOOT IT DOWN!! DO WHATEVER YOU MUST TO DESTROY THE AEGIS!!

I'VE NEVER HEARD OF SUCH A THING!

SHOT DOWN BY OUR OWN STOLEN WEAPONRY...!

A GINN UNIT HAS PENETRATED OUR FINAL LINE OF DEFENSE!!

DON'T BE RIDICULOUS!! UNDER THESE CIRCUM-STANCES...

VICE MINISTER ALLSTER, PLEASE GET ONBOARD THE LIFEPOD!

UWAAAAAA!!

!!

FLAY!!

SINCE THEN — JUST A TINY BIT OF TIME HAS ELAPSED —

ON THIS QUIET EVENING — I AWAIT YOUR RETURN —

AND THE MEMORIES — HAVE ONLY GOTTEN SWEETER TO THE LAST —

COME BACK — FOR THE SMILES — FROM THOSE TIMES — NOW FORGOTTEN

SZOO

HARO?

THE STARS —
......

?!

NOW I WILL DESTROY THEM, ONCE AND FOR ALL...

THEY'VE FINALLY TAKEN MY BAIT...

ONE MOBILE SUIT AND ONE MOBILE ARMOR!

HOW MANY?!

REIN-FORCE-MENTS, SIR!

VOOOOOOM

WH-WHAT'S THIS....?

ZU-ZU-ZU

SAVE MY DADDY! I'M BEGGING YOU!!

KID, PULL BACK AND TIGHTEN THE DEFENSES OF THE ARCHANGEL.

IT'S NEARLY DEMOL-ISHED...

DOSHOOM

F YOU AND GET SHOT DOWN, ALL IS LOST!!

STUPID KID!!

VOOOSH

KIRA
!!

THAT'S...
THE STRIKE!

DOSHOOM

STOP,
KIRA
!!

I DON'T WANT TO FIGHT YOU!!

BACK OFF, ATHRUN!!

WHY ARE YOU, A COORDINATOR, ALLYING YOURSELF WITH EARTH FORCES?!

YOU'RE THE ONE WHO SHOULD GIVE UP!!

BAM

BAM

BAM

BAM

BAM

AREN'T YOU THE ONE WHO WAS SO OPPOSED TO WAR?!

WHEN IT COMES TO MOBILITY, YOU'RE NO MATCH FOR THE AEGIS!

3 GINNS... AND THE X-303 AEGIS!

ENEMY STATUS?

ESCORT SHIP BERNARD AN LAW HAVE BEE DESTROYED. T MONTGOMERY SEVERELY DAM AGED.

DON'T BE RIDICU-LOUS!! THIS IS CREUSET WE'RE TALKING ABOUT!!

SEARCH HARDER !!

I CAN'T FIND IT!

MAYBE THEY'VE BEEN DESTROYED ...

THE CREUSET TEAM...?!

WHAT'S THE POSITION OF THE ENEMY SHIP?!

KABOOOM

THE MONTGOMERY IS DESTROYED!! THE ENTIRE ESCORT FLEET HAS BEEN OBLITERATED!!

HE PROMISED DADDY WOULD BE OKAY!!

NO... IT CAN'T BE...

O-OBLITERATED...?!

?!

GASP

HE PROMISED... ME...

FLAY!!

!!

3 GINNS ARE NOW APPROACH-ING THE ARCHANGEL !!

FLAY!! FLAY!!

.....

CAPTAIN! WE CAN'T JUST SIT HERE...!!

THE ARCHANGEL WILL WITHDRAW FROM THIS SECTOR!

I REALIZE THAT! CALL BACK THE STRIKE AND ZERO!

AND... THERE MAY BE AN ESCAPE POD THAT FLAY'S FATHER GOT ON...

IN THE MIDDLE OF BATTLE...?

COME BACK, KIRA!

IT'S UNLIKELY THEY WOULD HAVE BEEN ABLE TO LAUNCH AN ESCAPE POD UNDER SUCH CIRCUMSTANCES ...

!

KIRA!

WHE IS IT

ENEMY SHIP SIGHTED!!

COME BACK AT ONCE, KIRA YAMATO!!

BLAST! I CAN'T STOP THEM WITH THE ZERO ALONE!!

WH-WHAT'S THIS...THE ENEMY SHIP'S MAIN GUNS ARE LOCKED ONTO US!!

IT'S BEEN HIDING BEHIND THE DESTROYED ESCORT SHIP!!

WHAT?!

THERE'S NO TIME FOR THAT!!

EMERGENCY RETREAT!!

ATTENTION TO ZAFT SHIP! WE ARE CURRENTLY HOLDING MS. LACUS CLYNE ONBOARD THIS SHIP...

HE DAUGHTER OF SIEGEL CLYNE, SUPREME COUNCIL CHAIRMAN OF THE PLANT!

EH...?!

BY CHANCE, WE HAPPENED UPON HER LIFEPOD AND TOOK HER IN FOR HUMANITARIAN PURPOSES...

WHAT?!

A DIRTY TRICK!!

HMPH!

IF YOU PERSIST IN ATTACKING THIS SHIP, THE SAFETY OF MS. LACUS CANNOT BE GUARANTEED.

IS THIS YOUR SENSE OF JUSTICE, KIRA, FIGHTING ALONGSIDE SUCH TREACHEROUS COMPANY?!

COM-MANDER!!

OUR ARMY DOES NOT SUBMIT TO THREATS!

IF SHE IS THE DAUGHTER OF THE SUPREME COUNCIL CHAIRMAN, SHE SHOULD BE PREPARED TO DIE AN HONORABLE DEATH IN BATTLE RATHER THAN GO ON LIVING AS A PRISONER.

WE ARE PREPARED TO HAND OVER MS. LACUS IN EXCHANGE FOR A TEMPORARY CEASE-FIRE.

WE ARE NOT PIRATES!

VERY WELL... I SHALL DEFER TO YOUR SENSIBLE PROPOSAL.

WE CANNOT ALLOW OURSELVES TO BE MANIPULATED BY THEM.

WE ARE AT WAR, CAPTAIN.

SIR... I... I CANNOT CONDONE THIS SORT OF...

BUT FOR NOW, I WON'T ALLOW THE ARCHANGEL AND STRIKE TO BE DESTROYED!!

I'LL TAKE WHATEVER PUNISHMENT YOU GIVE LATER!!

ENSIGN BADGIRUEL!!

....

HARO?

DOES NOT COMPUTE.

.....?

THE STRIKE HAS RETURNED.

HARO.

HELLO?

JUST CHANG THE BATTER PACK!.

OK.

GET BEHIND ME.

I DON'T APRROVE OF USING HOSTAGES LIKE THIS, BUT...

THE AEGIS IS COMING TO PICK HER UP.

LIAR !!

I UNDER-STAND...

THERE'S NO TIME FOR ANYTHING ELSE!! DO THE REST LATER!!

WHY DIDN'T YOU SAVE DADDY!!

YOU PROMISED HE'D BE OKAY!!

HEY!

!!

YOU'RE JUST LIKE THEM! YOU'RE NOT REALLY FIGHTING THE COORDINATORS IN EARNEST, ARE YOU?!

......

CON-FIRMED...

DON'T LISTEN TO HER, KIRA-KUN...

COME BACK IMMEDIATELY AFTER YOU HAND LACUS OVER.

LAUNCH STRIKE!

OPEN THE HATCH!

BSHOOOM

BECAUSE...
I DON'T
WANT TO
FIGHT
ANYMORE.

WHY
ARE YOU
CRYING...?

?!

AND I
ESPECIALLY
DON'T WANT
TO FIGHT
AGAINST
ATHRUN...
AND YET...

I DON'T WANT
TO KILL OR BE
KILLED...

UWAA
AAAA
!!

?!

YOU KNOW ATHRUN?

ATHRUN'S MY FIANCÉ!

WOW.... REALLY?!

WE WERE BEST FRIENDS...

ATHRUN IS AN OLD FRIEND FROM MY LUNAR PREP SCHOOL DAYS...

.....

IT'S ALL SO... SAD.

BOTH YOU AND HE ARE SUCH GOOD PEOPLE...

PSHOO

KIRA....

ATHRUN...

KIRA.... KIRA YAMATO.

SORRY FOR THE TROUBLE I CAUSED...

...UM...

TAKE IT EASY...

THANK YOU, KIRA-SAMA... AND TAKE CARE.

LACUS... YOU MEAN SO MUCH TO ME...

I MISSED YOU SO MUCH!

I'M SO HAPPY TO SEE YOU, ATHRUN!

KIRA! COME WITH US!!

.....

?!

....

WHY REMAIN IN THE EARTH FORCES?!

IF NOT, I HAVE NO OTHER CHOICE B‍ TO SHOO‍ YOU DOWN!!

I TOO... HAVE NO WISH TO FIGHT YOU!

PHASE-07 END

EIGHTH FLEET SIGHTED UP AHEAD AT A DISTANCE OF 5000.

EH?!

I WANTED TO THANK YOU FOR ALL YOUR HARD WORK UP TILL NOW.

AFTER WE JOIN UP WITH THE FLEET, YOU WON'T HAVE TO PILOT THAT THING ANY LONGER.

.....

YEAH... I GUESS NOT.

WE ARE RECEIVING A TRANSMISSION FROM THE FLAGSHIP OF THE EIGHTH FLEET, MENELAOS.

SWITCHING TO VIDEO MONITOR.

IT'S GO TO SEE ADMI HALBER

I'M IMPRESSED YOU REACHED US SAFELY.

I OWE YOU MY THANKS, LIEUTENANT MURRUE.

BUT ON TO MORE PRESSING MATTERS. NOW THAT THE ARCHANGEL HAS FINISHED REFUELING...

YOU ARE TO LAND AT THE ALASKA HEAD-QUARTERS WITH YOUR ENTIRE CREW.

HOSE
RE THE
RDERS
ROM
NTRAL
OM-
AND.

MEANWHILE, THE CIVILIANS FROM HELIOPOLIS ARE TO BE TRANSPORTED BY SHUTTLE TO THE NATION OF AUBE.

NOT THE MOON... BUT ALASKA...?

IT'S TOO DANGEROUS!! WE CAN'T LAUNCH A DEFENSELESS SHUTTLE WHILE UNDER ATTACK BY ZAFT!!

AT'S
ULOUS!!
E'RE
OT—

THEY HAVE REQUESTED AN IMMEDIATE RELEASE OF ALL REFUGEES.

?!

THE AUBE NATION IS ACCUSING ARCHANGEL OF USING AUBE CIVILIANS AS HUMAN SHIELDS.

ZAFT IS STEPPING UP ITS OFFENSIVE.

WE TOO HAVE TO GET THE DEVELOPMENT OF THE "G" UNITS BACK ON TRACK.

I KNOW. I SUSPECT THE' ARE BEING PRESSURED BY ZAFT OPERATIVES.

THAT'S WHAT WE'RE HERE FOR.

WE WON'T LET ANYONE LAY A FINGER ON YOU!

BUT IF WE REENTER T ATMOSPHER THE ARCHANGE WILL ALSO DEFENSELES

ADMIRAL HALBERTON ...

!!

EVEN I THE ENTI EIGHT FLEET GOES DOWN THE PROCES

THE GAMOW AND ZIEGLER HAVE ARRIVED.

WHAT IS IT?

LOOK AT THIS, SIR.

BUT SOMETHING'S NOT QUITE RIGHT.

BUT JUDGING BY THEIR CURRENT COURSE, IT SEEMS LIKELY THAT THE LEGGED SHIP IS HEADED FOR EARTH.

HMMM.

THE LEGGED SHIP HAS MERGED WITH THE ENEMY FLEET. WE EXPECTED THEM TO HEAD FOR THE MOON BASE.

WHAT ...?

THE EIGHTH FLEET OF THE EARTH ALLIANCE IS UNDER THE COMMAND OF THE RENOWNED ADMIRAL HALBERTON.

WELL-VERSED IN THE USE OF MOBILE SUITS IN BATTLE.

THERE ARE 5 GINNS ONBOARD THE ZIEGLER, WHICH COMES TO A TOTAL OF 12 UNITS.

WHAT ABOUT OUR BATTLE STATUS?

HE MUST HAVE REALIZED THAT A BATTLESHIP AND MOBILE ARMOR ALONE AREN'T SUFFICIENT DEFENSES TO REACH THE MOON SAFELY.

YES SIR!

ATTACK THE LEGGED SHIP BEFORE IT REACHES EARTH!

PREPARE ALL UNITS FOR BATTLE.

IT'S TIME TO RETIRE OUR RENOWNED HALBERTON FROM THE GAME...

DUEL,
STER, AND
TZ, TO THE
ATAPULT
DECK
MEDIATELY!

READY TO
LAUNCH
MOBILE
SUITS.

IF WE LET HIM
GO THIS
TIME, WE
CAN'T VERY
WELL SHOW
OUR FACES
TO
COMMANDER
CREUSET,
CAN WE?

IT'S TIME TO
PAY THE
STRIKE
BACK FOR
OUR LAST
ENCOUNTER!

I'VE BEEN
WAITING
FOR THIS!

IF WE PURSUE
THEM TOO FAR,
WE'LL BE
SUCKED INTO
THE EARTH'S
GRAVITATIONAL
FIELD.

WE NEED
TO BE
EXTREMELY
CAREFUL,
THOUGH.

AEGIS,
PROCEED
TO CATA-
PULT
LAUNCH!

D-DISCHARGE PAPERS?!

I DIDN'T REALIZE WE WERE IN THE ARMY...

IN ORDER TO BYPASS THAT REGULATION...

ARRANGED ROACTIVELY THAT YOU LISTED AS OLUNTEERS OR TO THE STRUCTION HELIOPOLIS.

EVEN IN TIMES OF EMERGENCY IT IS ILLEGAL FOR CIVILIANS TO PARTICIPATE IN MILITARY ACTION.

!!

NO WAY....

.....

WAIT!!

THE SHUTTLE FOR AUBE WILL BE LEAVING SHORTLY.

PACK UP YOUR THINGS.

HM?!

I...

I VOLUNTE FOR TH EARTH FORCES

I WANT TO STAY ON THIS SHIP!!

FLAY...

IF NOT, I'LL NEVER FORGIVE YOU!!

FIGHT THOSE COORDINA- TORS, THEY WHO ARE JUST LIKE YOU, AND FIGHT THEM TO THE DEATH!!

YOU COULDN'T EVEN SAVE DADDY AND YOU PLAN ON LEAVING THIS SHIP!! HOW DARE YOU!!

!

YOU SHOULD VOLUNTEER TOO!!

?!

HEY, MISTER

UH-HUH.

IS THAT... FOR ME ...?

THANK YOU FOR PROTECT- ING US.

AN EMERGENCY TRANSMISSION FROM THE CAPTAIN OF THE MENELAOS!!

ALL HANDS, ASSUME PRIMARY BATTLE STATIONS!!

ENEMY MOBILE SUITS APPROACHING!!

YOU WILL NOT TAKE PART IN COMBAT, BUT INSTEAD WILL PREPARE FOR REENTRY INTO THE ATMOSPHERE!

LIEUTENANT RAMIUS, AFTER LAUNCHING THE REFUGEE SHUTTLE, YOU ARE TO TAKE UP THE REAR OF THE FLEET.

WE WILL NOT LET A SINGLE SHIP PASS, UPON THE HONOR OF THE EIGHTH FLEET.

IT IS NOT YOUR RESPONSI-BILITY TO ENGAGE THE ENEMY!!

B-BUT....

BLIP

WHAT ARE YOU DOING HERE?!

?!

SORRY WE'RE LATE!

THEY'VE VOLUNTEERED.

IT'S AN EMERGENCY, SO I GAVE MY CONSENT.

ENSIGN BADGIRUEL...

WE CAN'T JUST LEAVE FLAY BY HERSELF, AFTER ALL.

SHE'S OUR FRIEND...

IS THIS REALLY THE RIGHT CHOICE?

?!

YEAH... I GUESS YOU'RE RIGHT...

BESIDES, I KIND OF AGREE WITH WHAT FLAY SAID.

DOOOM

LAUNCHING REFUGEE SHUTTLE!

NO...THIS SIGNAL IS...

A MOBILE SUIT?!

A VESSEL HAS LAUNCHED FROM THE LEGGED SHIP!

WHAT?! A
REFUGEE
SHIP HAS
LEFT THE
LEGGED
SHIP?!

O, DON'T
WORRY
BOUT IT.

SHALL I
INTERCEPT
THE SHIP?

STRANGE,
CONSIDERING
THE TIMING...

AND AT THIS
POINT, I
DOUBT IF
IT'S A
TRICK.
LEAVE IT BE.

OUR
ATTACK
PLAN IS
ALREADY
UNDER WAY.

VOOOOSH

HMPH...

ONCE THE ENEMY IS DISPERSED, WE CAN TAKE THEM OUT ONE BY ONE!!

ASSUME PHALANX FORMATION AND HIT THEM WITH EVERYTHING WE'VE GOT!!

ALL SHIPS, OPEN FIRE!!

ENEMY MOBILE SUIT TEAM APPROACHING AT A DISTANCE OF 5000.

FIRE!!

KA-BLAM

BLAM

BLAM

KACHOOOM

LANDING ENGINES AT 40%.

ERROR MARGIN OF ENTRY VECTOR SET AT 2-DEGREE ANGLE OF DEPRESSION.

VOOOOOOOM

WHERE ARE YOU, STRIKE?!

THE BATTLE ONLY STARTED LESS THAN TEN MINUTES AGO...

WHAT IS IT?

I... CAN'T BELIEVE IT...

!!

YET THERE'S NO RESPONSE FROM NEARLY HALF THE FLEET...

?!

LAUNCH US AT THE LAST SECOND!!

CAPTAIN!

ADMIRAL HALBERTON...

AT THIS RATE, THE ARCHANGEL WON'T MAKE IT!!

WHAT ARE YOU TALKING ABOUT, LIEUTENANT FLAGA?!

KIRA-KUN...YOU VOLUNTEERED TOO...?!

ACCORDING TO ITS CATALOG SPECS, THE STRIKE CAN MAKE A SOLO LANDING.

?!

ATHRUN, HAVE YOU NOTICED?!

ZU-ZU-ZU-ZU

KIRA...!

YES... STRIKE AND THE MOBILE ARMOR AREN'T HERE...

UNLESS...

WHY HAVEN'T THEY LAUNCHED?!

YZAK, WHERE ARE YOU GOING?!

VOOOM

AN UNDER-HANDED PLOY!!

THE ENEMY IS USING THE REFUGEE SHIP AS A DECOY SO THAT THE STRIKE CAN LAND ON THE SURFACE BY ITSELF!!

RETURN TO SHIP 3 MINUTES AFTER ATTACK, KIRA!

STRIKE, PROCEED TO CATAPULT LAUNCH!

ROGER!

DON'T EVEN THINK ABOUT REENTERING THE ATMOSPHERE ALONE! NO ONE HAS EVER DONE IT BEFORE!

VOHHHH

!!

DUEL IS HEADED FOR THE REFUGEE SHIP!!

WHAT ?!

?!

THAT'S... THE STRIKE?!

I'M GETTING HEAVIER AND HEAVIER!

AND I'M JUST A HAIR'S BREADTH AWAY FROM THE ARCHANGEL!

WHOOOSH

HOW UNEXPECTED ...

?!

BSHOOM

DON'T YOU TOUCH THAT SHIP!!

WHAT'S THAT?!... BEHIND ME?!

VSSHH

KRAKK!

UWAAA AAA.!!

!!

BASHOO

ATHRUN! THE GAMOW, IT'S...

YZAK, ARE YOU ALL RIGHT ?!

BOOM ズ BOOM ズ BOOM ズ BOOM

BADOOOOM

CHANK

ADMIRAL HALBERTON ....!

!! THE MENELAOS HAS BEEN DESTROYED !!

WE ARE NOW PASSING THROUGH THE ATMOSPHERIC REENTRY THRESHOLD.

ZERO HAS ATTACHED ITSELF TO THE SHIP!!

WHOOOSHH

HOW ABOUT IT, BUSTER! NOW YOU CAN'T GO BACK!!

WELL... HE HASN'T COME BACK YET.

WHAT ABOUT THE KID?!

UGHH... MOVE IT, BUSTER! MOVE!!

SHOOOOM!

WHAT ?!

WHAT'S WRONG, YZAK?!

VOOOOOSHH

KIRA... KIRA! CO[ME] BACK T[O] THE SHIP

THE CONTROLS... THEY'RE NOT RESPONDING....

KIRA... STRI...

KRAK KRAK...

COME BA—

YZ... AK...

KRAK KRAK...

OWWW... OWWW...!!

AS FOR DEARKA AND YZAK... THERE'S NOTHING WE CAN DO FOR THEM NOW...

BRING BACK ATHRUN AND NICOL AT ONCE!

EH?!

?!

CURSE YOU, STRIKE !!

WHY... WHY DID YOU HAVE TO RUIN EVERY- THING... ?!

ZZZN

NOOO OOO !!

!!

SHOOOM

BABOOOM

PHASE-08 END

GET CLOSER TO STRIKE!! WE MAY BE ABLE TO REACH HIM IN TIME WITH THE ARCHANGEL'S THRUSTERS!!

OUR ENTRY VECTOR IS MISALIGNED WITH THE STRIKE'S! AT THIS RATE, HE'LL MISS THE DROP POINT!!

HURRY!!

IF WE LOSE THE STRIKE, NONE OF THAT MATTERS!!

IN ALASKA ...!!

BUT THEN WE'LL MISS THE DROP POINT TOO...

VOOOOOM

KIRA!... ARE YOU OKAY... KIRA...?!

CHANK

STRIKE ATTACHING TO SHIP... CONFIRMED!!

?!

THANK GOD.... YOU'RE AWAKE!

UGHHH...!

OU'VE EEN EP FOR E DAYS OW.

FLAY....

I SAID SOME TERRIBLE THINGS TO YOU BEFORE, KIRA... SO... I KNOW IT'S INEXCUSABLE, BUT...

WE'RE IN THE DESERT ON EARTH. SOME- WHERE ON THE AFRICAN CONTINENT APPARENTLY ...

CAREFUL... DON'T GET UP YET!

BUT WHY ARE YOU...?! WHERE AM I...?

?!

I'M SORRY! FOR SAYING THAT YOU WEREN'T FIGHTING IN EARNEST...

IT'S OKAY... DON'T WORRY ABOUT IT...

!!

IT'S...

THANK YOU FOR PROTECTING US.

-UGHHH
...

KIRA...?

KIRA....

OOHHH...

THAT LITTLE GIRL... I... COULDN'T SAVE HER...

?

I'LL TAKE CARE OF YOU...

IT'S OKAY, KIRA. I'M HERE.

THAT'S RIGHT, EVERYONE'S BEEN ROMOTED... HA HA HA...

OH... YOU MEANT ME WHEN YOU SAID "OFFICER"...?

?!

HEY, ARE YOU LISTENING TO ME, PETTY OFFICER MURDOCH?!

BUT THAT OESN'T MEAN THINGS ARE GONNA GET EASY FROM NOW ON...

I'M GRATEFUL FOR ADMIRAL HALBERTON'S GOOD FAVOR...

ALLY...

THEY WERE TALKING ABOUT HIM UP IN THE BRIDGE.

THAT'S THE NAME OF THE UNDEFEATED ZAFT COMMANDER OF AFRICA.

WE NOW HAVE TO FACE THE "DESERT TIGER."

JUST WHEN WE THOUGHT WE ESCAPED FROM THE CREUSET TEAM...

UTENANT MU LA LAGA!

SO WHAT MADE US LAND IN A PLACE LIKE THIS...?

THE TIGER?

THERE YOU GO... SPEAK OF THE DEVIL!

PLEASE RETURN T[THE BRIDGE AT ONCE! LIEUTENAN[FLAGA, TO THE BRIDGE AT ONC[

?!

NO... IT'S NOT THAT...

WHAT'S WRONG? THE ENEMY?!

WE JUST RECEIVED A TRANSMISSION FROM THEM...

A LOCAL RESISTANCE GROUP CALLED "DESERT DAWN" WISHES TO MEET WITH US.

ダ ダ
TONK

TONK

DESER[DAWN?

THANK YOU...

WE ARE DESERT DAWN. FIRST OFF, WE'D LIKE TO THANK YOU FOR PERMITTING US TO MEET WITH YOU.

I'LL HAVE YOU KNOW THAT WE ARE NOT ZAFT, BUT THAT DOESN'T MAKE US YOUR ALLIES EITHER!

I'M THE LEADER OF DESERT DAWN, SAHIB ASHMAN.

SO IF [YO]U PLAN ON [T]AKING ON [T]HE TIGER, WE'LL [CO]OPERATE [WITH] YOU.

BUT OUR CURRENT ENEMY IS THE DESERT TIGER.

THE WAY WE SEE IT, ZAFT AND THE EARTH ALLIANCE ARE ONE AND THE SAME!

[O]R AM I [MIS]TAKEN?

ANOTHER WAY OF LOOKING AT IT IS YOU'RE JUST TRYING TO USE US TO DEFEAT THIS TIGER.

BOTH SIDES JUST COME TO CONTROL US AND STEAL FROM US.

THEN WE'LL TREAT YOU JUST LIKE THE TIGER: AS OUR ENEMY!

AND DESTROY YOU WITHOUT HESITATION!

AND IF WE REFUSE?

THERE'S NO WAY YOU CAN LEAVE THIS SECTOR WITHOUT FIGHTING THE TIGER.

?!

YOU HEARD 'IM....

JUST AS I THOUGHT. THE X-105 STRIKE...

.....

.....

.....

FLAY... WHAT ARE YOU DOING?

NONE OF MY BUSINESS ...!

N-NONE OF MY BUSINESS ...?!

SAI, IT'S NONE OF YOUR BUSINESS.

LET ME GO!!

YOU'RE KIDDING, RIGHT?! YOU'RE JOKING, FLAY!!

L-LET HER GO, SAI...

CLENCH

SAI!

KIRA!!

JUST THE WAY I WANT IT...THE RISK WAS WORTH IT...

....

HE'LL DO IT TO PROTECT ME...HE'LL FIGHT AND HE'LL FIGHT...AND AVENGE MY DADDY'S DEATH...

KIRA WILL STICK WITH THE ARCHANGEL AND FIGHT AGAINST HIS FELLOW COORDINATORS ...

THAT GUY...?! FROM HELIOPOLIS ...

I BETTER LAUNCH THE STRIKE!

YOU HAVEN'T RECEIVED LAUNCH CLEARANCE YET!!

THE OBJECTIVE IS TO GAUGE THE FIGHTING CAPACITY OF THE ENEMY SHIP AND ITS MOBILE SUIT.

BE CAREFUL! THERE MAY BE A SEPARATE DETACHMENT HIDING SOME- WHERE!!

ONLY TWO...?!

CONFIRMED AS ZAFT FORCES TMF/A-802 BuCUE TYPES!!

TWO ENEMY MOBILE SUITS!!

WAIT! IT'S NOT YET CLEAR HOW MANY ENEMY FORCES THERE ARE!

BRIDGE! OPEN THE HATCH, QUICKLY!!

CONFIRMED!

VOHHHH

DON'T BE IMPULSIVE AND RUSH INTO BATTLE!

THIS ISN'T THE TIME TO WORRY ABOUT THAT CRAP!

I DON'T LIKE YOUR TONE OF VOICE, ENSIGN YAMATO.

BUT YOU DO HAVE A POINT...

WE'VE GOTTA LAUNCH THE STRIKE NOW!

WHAT'S THE STATUS OF LIEUTENANT FLAGA'S SKY-GRASPER?!

LAUNCH THE STRIKE!!

SHHOO

ZZUN

EH?!

BUT HERE IN THE DESERT THE BuCUE IS KING!!

THOOOM

MAYBE IT'S DIFFERENT IN SPACE...

THOOOM

UWAA!!

THOOC

IT'S A SITTING DUCK OUT THERE!!

BRING BACK THE STRIKE!!

BLAM

BLAM

BLAM

UWAAA AAA!!

BLAM

THEY'RE COMING... THE BuCUES... THEY'LL DESTROY US... THE STRIKE... AND THE ARCHANGEL TOO...

STRIKE, RETURN TO THE ARCHANGEL AT ONCE!

I CAN'T LET ANYONE DIE ANYMORE!!

BZOOO

I WON'T LET ANYONE DIE!!

K-CHAK

KCHOOOM

DOOM

DOOM

DOOM

DOOM

HIT HIM WHEN HIS BALANCE IS OFF, JUST AS HE DROPS DOWN!!

?!

ZZUN

N!!

KTHOOM

KA-BOOOOOM

THONK

WHOMP

BLAM

AAAA
AA!!

MEIMU-RAAAA!!

BLAST! WHERE IS HE?!

IMPOSSIBLE...

THAT MOBILE SUIT...ADJUSTED ITS MOTOR PROGRAM TO DESERT CONDITIONS IN SUCH A SHORT TIME...?

HE USED THE SHOCKWAVE TO JUMP UP TO A HIGH ALTITUDE?!

THOOOM

!!

BLAMM

KA-BOOOM

MY GOD...

OOOOH...

CRAP...!

....

HE'S
INCREDIBLE
...

.....

YOU'RE... THE GIRL FROM HELIOPOLIS...?!

PLEASE ACCEPT MY APOLOGY FOR LOSING THE TWO BuCUE UNITS YOU PROVIDED ME WITH...

QUITE INTERESTING, REALLY... ESPECIALLY THAT MOBILE SUIT... AND ITS PILOT...

YOU GATHERED IMPORTANT DATA THAT WAS WORTH THE LOSS...

DON'T WORRY ABOUT IT, DACOSTA-KUN.

PHASE-09 END

PHASE-10 THE FANGS OF THE NEMESIS

HOW COME YOU'RE PILOTING THAT THING?!

I'M ASKING YOU WHY YOU'RE PILOTING THAT THING!!

YOU'RE THE GIRL FROM HELIOPOLIS...

I... HAD NO CHOICE...

.....

WHAT DO YOU MEAN, YOU HAD NO CHOICE?!

WHAT?!

BUT... THERE AREN'T ANY SHELTERS LEFT...

WHAT ABOUT YOU...?!

C'MON, GET INSIDE!

I'LL BE FINE, NOW GO...

SZZOO

WHAM

?!

IS THAT WHAT YOU'RE SAYING ?!

YOU'RE PILOTING A MOBILE SUIT AND WAGING WAR BECAUSE YOU "HAD NO CHOICE"?!

WH-WHAT'RE YOU...?!

HEY, YOU TWO, STOP!

SHUU

SHUT UP!! YOU HAVE NO IDEA WHAT I'VE BEEN THROUGH SINCE HELIOPOLIS...

WELL, WHAT DO YOU THINK YOU'RE DOING HERE...?

NOTHING... REALLY...

WHAT DID YOU SAY TO HER?!

CLENCH

CALM DOWN, CAGALLI!!

LET ME GO!!

HOW'S THE CONDITION OF THIS SHIP?

THE BuCUES WERE DEFEATED... BUT THE TIGER WON'T TAKE THAT SITTING DOWN!

WHO WOULD HAVE THOUGHT THOSE TWO KNEW EACH OTHER...

SO WE DON'T HAVE MUCH LEEWAY IN TERMS OF SUPPLIES.

WE ORIGINALLY PLANNED TO DROP DOWN IN ALASKA...

THE BIGGER PROBLEM IS THE TIGER.

BUT THIS IS ZAFT TERRITORY!

IT'S NOT GOING TO BE EASY...

THEN YO BETTER RESUPPL FIRST.

?

HUH...?

I'M NOT THAT HAPPY ABOUT IT, BUT...

MAYB BUT I H AN ID

ALL RIGHT, YOU'VE GOT FOUR HOURS...

I SEE....

THE CAPTAIN GAVE HER APPROVAL.

BESIDES, PROTECTING HER IS AN IMPORTANT JOB.

FOR ME TO LEAVE THE SHIP LIKE THIS...?

BUT IS IT REALLY OKAY?

I WAS JUST SO SHOCKED THAT YOU WERE THE PILOT OF THAT THING...

?!

SORRY ABOUT YESTERD...

YEAH... EVEN I CAN'T BELIEVE EVERYTHING THAT'S HAPPENED...

IT'S THE TIME WE LIVE IN. THINGS HAV BEEN TOUGH FOR BOTH O US...

BUT THE VALUE OF THE EQUIPMENT THEY SELL IS UNDENIABLE.

I'M NOT TOO FOND OF ARMS TRADERS...

?!

BY THE W WONDER NATARLE ARE REAL GONNA ALL RIGH

AND SAHIB IS WITH THEM, SO THEY'LL BE FINE.

SO LET'S EAT!

WELL, WE'VE FINISHED MOST OF OUR SHOPPING.

CAGALLI... WHAT ARE THESE...?

?!

THEY'RE KEBABS! YOU NEVER HEARD OF THEM?... WELL, THAT'S WHAT YOU GET FOR BEING IN A SPACE SHIP FOR SO LONG...

?!

BOOM

IT'S A COORDI-NATOR!!

WAM

COSTA-KUN! CLEAN THEM UP FOR ME.

THE BLUE COSMOS ...?!

FOR THE BLUE EARTH, FREE FROM IMPURITIES !!

GO TO HELL, BACK WHERE YOU CAME FROM !!

LOOK OUT !!

KICK

HUH?!

BOP

?!

THOKK

CURSE YOU... DESERT... TIGER...

SURE. NO PROBLEM.

ARE YOU ALL RIGHT, COMMANDER?

HMPH....

?!

ANDREW WALTFELD OF ZAFT?!

DESERT TIGER?!

RELAX. MAKE YOURSELVES AT HOME.

WHAT BUSINESS DOES THE DESERT TIGER HAVE WITH US?!

YOU CAN'T GO HOME LOOKING LIKE THAT.

THE LEAST I CAN DO IS HAVE YOUR CLOTHES CLEANED...

THE TWO OF YOU WERE INCONVENIENC[ED] BECAUSE OF M[E]

AH!

COME ON.... LET'S GO.

.....

HOW WOULD YOU LIKE SOME COFFEE?

DON'T WORRY. AISHA WILL TAKE GOOD CARE OF HER.

MOCHA SIDAMO IS KNOWN AS THE "GRANDE DAME OF COFFEE." IT'S THE HIGHEST QUALITY MOCHA.

I TRIED BLENDING MOCHA SIDAMO WITH 10% SANTOS NO. 2.

?

DELICIOUS ...

!

IT'S JUST A TAD BITTER

!!

AND RECENTLY, THE ONLY NEWCOMER HAS BEEN THE EARTH FORCES' NEW BATTLESHIP...

I KNOW EVERYONE IN THIS TOWN... WHEN A STRANGER COMES, IT'S PRETTY OBVIOUS.

ONLY A COORDINATOR COULD FIGHT LIKE THAT.

NOT TO MENTION THE PILOT OF THAT MOBILE SUIT WHO REPROGRAMMED HIS SOFTWARE IN A MOMENT'S NOTICE TO ADJUST TO THE SAND PRESSURE ...

CLICK

RELAX. I WON'T DO ANYTHING TO YOU NOW.

TMP

TELL ME, HOW DO YOU PLAN ON PUTTING AN END TO THIS WAR?

D-DON'T PATRONIZE ME!

WHAT ARE YOU TRYING TO SAY?!

HOW....

BY KILLING ALL OF THE ENEMY?

!!

EH?

BUT WHEN WE MEET ON THE BATTLEFIELD, IT'LL BE DIFFERENT, KID.

.....

I'LL SHOW YOU OUT.

GIBRALTAR BASE,
ZAFT FORCES

YZAK AND DEARK
I'M SO PLEASED
THAT BOTH OF YO
HAVE LANDED ON
EARTH SAFELY.

THERE WILL SOON
BE A CLEAN-UP
OPERATION OF THE
RESISTANCE AND
THE LEGGED SHIP.

I REALIZE YOU
MUST BE TIRED,
BUT I WANT YOU
TO MERGE WITH
THE WALTFELD
TEAM.

....

WELL-WELL...
SO WE'RE
NOT ALLOWED
TO RETURN
TO SPACE...

YESSIR

THAT'S
FINE
WITH
ME!

AND I'LL DO IT WITH MY REBORN DUEL... THE NEW ASSAULT SHROUD!

THERE'S A DEBT TO BE REPAID FOR MY INJURIES!

CONTINUED IN VOLUME 3

A Brief History of Gundam
Part 2: The Themes of *Gundam SEED*
By Mark Simmons

In the *Gundam SEED* television series, director Mitsuo Fukuda set out to reinvent the original Mobile Suit Gundam for the twenty-first century. The visual differences are immediately apparent, as *Gundam SEED* is packed with complex, detailed machinery, and the characters—designed for the animated series by Hisashi Hirai, and reinterpreted here by artist Masatsugu Iwase—have the sleek, stylized look of modern anime. The dialogue, with its abundance of military and technological jargon, also contributes to the atmosphere of realism. In addition to these stylistic elements, the creators also made some topical changes to the story's underlying themes to update the classic *Gundam* premise for a new era...

A New Breed

For twenty-five years, the Gundam saga has returned again and again to the premise of a conflict between Earth and its rebel space colonies. Usually, these struggles are purely political in nature, with a population of space colonists growing tired of living under the control of distant rulers and launching a war of independence, not unlike the American Revolution.

In *Gundam SEED*, however, the war is also an ethnic conflict of sorts, fought between genetically engineered Coordinators and unmodified Naturals. The Coordinators made a new home in the space colonies to escape the jealousy and persecution of the Naturals, only to find themselves in economic bondage to the Earth nations which funded the construction of the colonies. This war of independence is thus the end result of genetic discrimination, and the differences between the two sides are a matter not just of where they live, but of who they are. As the fighting escalates, radicals on both sides hope to bring about a clash of civilizations that will leave only one human species.

The concept of the Coordinators, a new breed of humanity with amazing mental and physical abilities, also echoes previous Gundam series. According to Gundam lore, the new environment of outer space may bring about a new stage in human evolution, represented by so-called Newtypes with vastly expanded powers of awareness and intuition. But *Gundam SEED's* Coordinators have no such spiritual gifts, and since their superhuman abilities are the product of artificial genetic modification, they are children of science rather than of natural evolution.

Uneasy Alliances

Gundam SEED also reflects the modern era in its complex political setup. While previous series assumed that the Earth of the future would inevitably be ruled by a single world government along the lines of the United Nations, in *Gundam SEED* the Earth Alliance which represents the Naturals is actually a joint enterprise of several different terrestrial superpowers, which scheme against each other even as they cooperate against the Coordinators.

The Atlantic Federation, based in North America, is the leading power of the Alliance and the creator of the prototype Gundams. Among its rivals are the Eurasian Federation, which corresponds to Russia and the modern-day European Union, and the Republic of East Asia, made up of China, Japan, and Korea. Earth is also home to countless smaller nations, of which some side with the Coordinators and others remain strictly neutral.

Weapons of War

The humanoid fighting vehicles known as mobile suits are another mainstay of the Gundam saga. Although the mobile suits of *Gundam SEED* are superficially similar to those of earlier series, their technological basis is rather different. Thanks to the widespread use of devices called Neutron Jammers, which suppress all forms of nuclear fission, these mobile suits rely on batteries for their power supply. For the prototype Gundams, with their energy-guzzling beam weapons and bulletproof Phase Shift Armor, this power limitation proves to be a recurring Achilles heel.

Continued in Volume 3!

Coming from Del Rey Manga December 2004.

About the Creators

Yoshiyuki Tomino

Gundam was created by Yoshiyuki Tomino. Prior to Gundam, Tomino had worked on the original *Astro Boy* anime, as well as *Princess Knight* and *Brave Raideen*, among others. In 1979, he created and directed *Mobile Suit Gundam*, the very first in a long line of Gundam series. The show was not immediately popular and was forced to cut its number of episodes before going off the air, but as with the American show *Star Trek*, the fans still had something to say on the matter. By 1981, the demand for Gundam was so high that Tomino oversaw the re-release of the animation as three theatrical movies (a practice still common in Japan, and rarely if ever seen in the U.S.). It was now official: Gundam was a blockbuster.

Tomino would go on to direct many Gundam series, including *Gundam ZZ*, *Char's Counterattack*, *Gundam F91* and *Victory Gundam*, all of which contributed to the rich history of the vast Gundam universe. In addition to Gundam, Tomino created *Xabungle*, *L. Gaim*, *Dunbine*, and *Garzey's Wing*. His most recent anime is *Brain Powered*, which was released by Geneon in the United States.

Masatsugu Iwase

Masatsugu Iwase writes and draws the manga adaptation of *Gundam SEED*. It is his first work published in the U.S. The manga creator is better known in Japan, however, for his work on *Calm Breaker*, a hilarious parody of anime, manga, and Japanese pop culture.

Translation Notes

Japanese is a tricky language for most Westerners, and translation is often more art than science. For your edification and reading pleasure, here are notes on some of the places where we could have gone in a different direction in our translation of the work, or where a Japanese cultural reference is used.

Yo, Dirtbag!

In this panel, Flay is calling Tolle a "hentai" in Japanese. A "hentai" is someone who is perverted or twisted, but the term pervert usually has different connotations in English. So instead of going with "Tolle, you're a pervert!" the translator thought "dirtbag" would be more appropriate here.

And Not a Drop to Drink

We have quite a few proverbs and sayings in English that would make no sense if translated literally into a foreign language. The same holds true for Japanese. Sai is quoting a Japanese proverb here. "Se ni hara wa kaerarenai" literally means "You can't change your back for your stomach." In other words: "You can't have it both ways." In the current context, the translator thought "We really have no choice" would make more sense.

I Will Bother You

In English, we have greetings that aren't meant to be taken literally. For example, saying "How do you do?" when meeting someone is not a question meant to be taken literally and is usually met with the response "Fine." Here, Lacus is using the Japanese expression "Ojama shimasu," which is pretty much untranslatable. It literally

means "I will bother you," or more loosely, "Sorry to disturb you." In Japan, before entering someone else's home or personal space (such as a car, a room, or an office), one frequently says "Ojama shimasu." It's used so often in Japan that it's become a greeting more than anything else, which is why the translator chose to translate it as "Hello" in this context.

The Legged Ship

HMMM.

THE LEGGED SHIP HAS MERGED WITH THE ENEMY FLEET. WE EXPECTED THEM TO HEAD FOR THE MOON BASE.

In Japanese, the Zaft frequently refer to the Archangel as the "Ashi-tsuki" which literally means "legged" or something that has legs. In the beginning, it's because they don't know its name. Later on, even after they find out it's called the Archangel, they (especially Rau) refer to it as "the legged ship" with a "you're not important enough for me to use your real name" kind of attitude. This is similar to how the Zeons kept calling the White Base "the Trojan" in the original *Mobile Suit Gundam*.

WAM!

BUT WHO IS IT THAT HAS BRUTALLY SMASHED THAT HOPE?!

Wam Bam Thank You...

Sound effects remain one of the most difficult elements of manga to translate. In English, we expect sound effects to be onomatopoeic—to resemble the sounds they're making. In Japanese, the effects are more subtle and complex. Here are two examples: First, on page 35 Zala stands up abruptly to make his point more forcefully. The effect can actually be translated as "the sense of standing suddenly."

And on page 170, as these three men stand up with guns drawn, the effect can be translated as "giving the sense of taking out their guns."

IT'S A COORDI-NATOR!!

WAM

Preview of Volume Three

We are pleased to present to you a preview from *Gundam SEED*, Volume 3. This volume is available in bookstores now.

DON'T LET THEIR MAIN MOBILE SUIT GET ANY CLOSER TO US!!

INITIATE AIR-BORNE DEFENSE !!

THE ENEMY'S BATTLESHIPS AND MOBILE SUITS ARE APPROACHING! !

THAT'S AN ORDER! DON'T LET THEM DIE IN VAIN.

BUT...

I'LL BUY THEM SOME TIME TO PULL BACK.

DACOSTA-KUN, AS SOON AS I'M OUT THERE, GIVE OUR REMAINING FORCES THE ORDER TO RETREAT.

CLICK

WALTFELD TAKING OFF!!

ROARRRR

コゴゴゴゴ

BLAM

THAT'S NOT A BuCUE...THAT'S THE GENERAL'S SHIP..COULD IT BE HIM!?

WHAT THE !?...

HE'S GOT SHARP INSTINCTS.

HE DODGED US...

HE'S A WORTHY OPPONENT!!

ANDY, IT'S FROM THAT KID...

WE'RE RECEIVING AN ELECTRONIC TRANSMIS- SION.

BUT...

HE'S A SKILLED PILOT... AND HIS JUDGMENT IS PERFECT.

STOP IT PLEASE, WALTFELD- SAN!!

THE BATTLE IS OVER!!

NEGIMA!
VOLUME 2
BY KEN AKAMATSU

For ten-year-old teacher Negi Springfield and his all-girl class, it's time for final exams! If his students manage not to end up with the lowest scores in school, the principal has promised to make Negi an official teacher. To prepare for the tests, the class takes a trip to the school's Library Island. But this is no quiet place of study . . . stone golems, traps, and secret passageways are the norm throughout the enormous library building. With all of these distractions, can Negi's class hope to climb out of the cellar—both academically and literally?

Volumes 1-7 are now available in bookstores.

For more information and to sign up for Del Rey's manga e-newsletter, visit www.delreymanga.com

Finished already?
Try these titles from
Del Rey!

TOMARE!

[STOP!]

You're going the wrong way!

Manga is a completely different type of reading experience.

To start at the *beginning,* go to the *end*!

That's right! Authentic manga is read the traditional Japanese way—from right to left. Exactly the *opposite* of how American books are read. It's easy to follow: Just go to the other end of the book, and read each page—and each panel—from right side to left side, starting at the top right. Now you're experiencing manga as it was meant to be.